Left foot
Left foot

Right foot
Right

Feet in the morning

Feet at night

Left foot

Left foot

Left foot

Right

Wet foot

Dry foot

High foot

Low foot

Front feet

Back feet

Red feet

Black feet

Left foot          Right foot

Feet          Feet          Feet

How many, many
feet you meet.

Slow feet

Quick feet

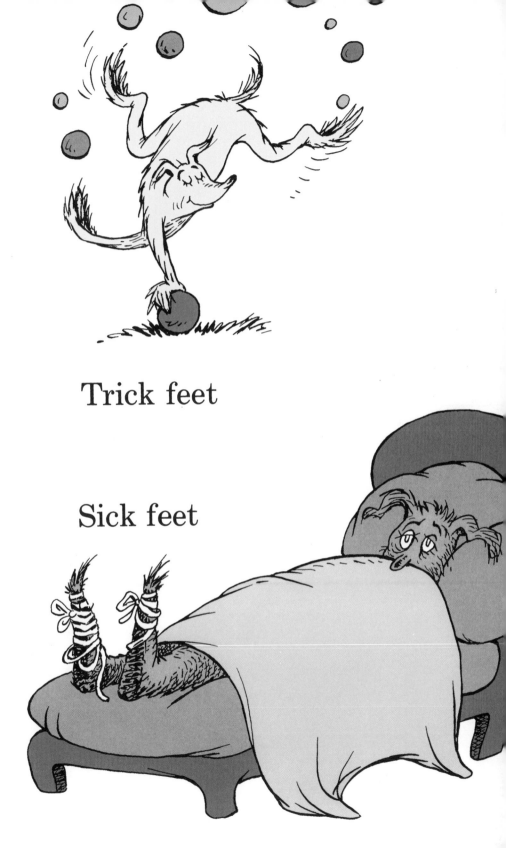

Trick feet

Sick feet

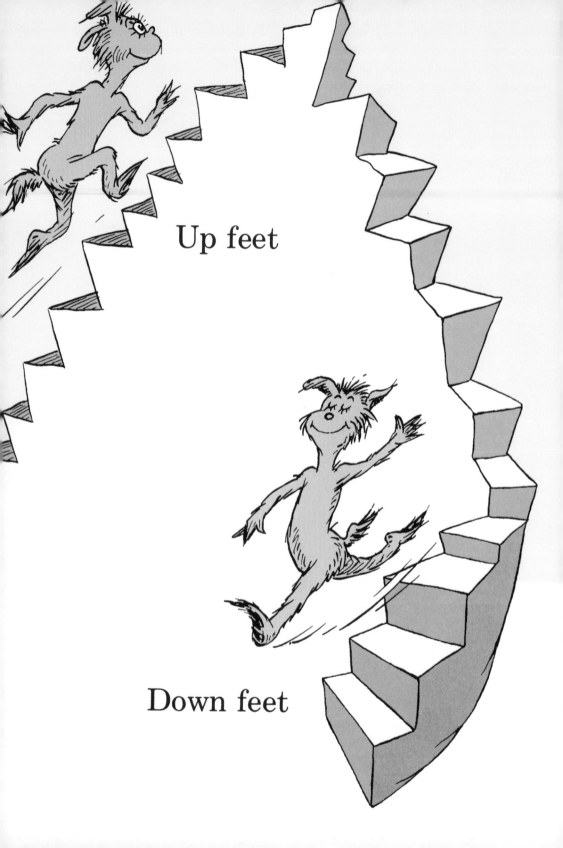

Up feet

Down feet

Here come clown feet.

Small feet

Big feet

Here come pig feet.

His feet

Her feet

Fuzzy fur feet

In the house,
and on the street,

how many, many
feet you meet.

Up in the air feet

Over a chair feet

# More and more feet

Twenty-four feet

Here come
more and more . . . . . . . . . . . .

. . . . . . . . and more feet!

Left foot.      Right foot.

Feet. Feet. Feet.

Oh, how many
feet you meet!